For Joseph, Brune and Siméon.
With thanks to Mole.
A. D.

Translated from the French by Claudia Zoe Bedrick

enchantedlion.com

First published in 2015 by Enchanted Lion Books,
351 Van Brunt Street, Brooklyn, NY 11231

Originally published in French as *Edmond, la fête sous la lune*
Copyright © 2013, Editions Nathan, Paris – France
Copyright © 2015 by Enchanted Lion Books for the English-language translation

ISBN 978-1-59270-174-2

All rights reserved under International and Pan-American Copyright Conventions
A CIP record is on file with the Library of Congress

Printed in France

First Printing

Astrid Desbordes   Marc Boutavant

Edmond
The moonlit party

ENCHANTED LION BOOKS

NEW YORK

Edmond the squirrel lived in a house that was small and neat, just like him. It was a pleasant place, nestled in the trunk of an old chestnut tree, and because Edmond was timid, he hardly ever went out.

Instead, he made nut jam, read adventure stories, and spent his evenings making pompoms.

Edmond was an amazing pompom maker and could finish a magnificent pompom hat in no more than a day or two.

So he often thought that making pompoms was what suited him best of all.

Mr. George Owl lived above Edmond, at the top of the old chestnut tree. Unlike Edmond, George was always outside. He spent his days collecting feathers, moss, leaves, bark— anything he could use in a costume, because disguising himself was George's favorite thing in the whole world. His house was full of costumes, each in its own box: rhinoceros, tarantula, polar bear, the very fuzzy polar bear, beaver, falcon, lizard, whale, and more.

The other forest animals often crossed paths with George when he was disguised, perhaps as a ladybug or maybe a hedgehog, but they hardly ever recognized him.

Harry the bear lived at the bottom of the old chestnut tree. He was known throughout the forest for the parties he threw each season. As soon as he announced a party, no one would talk of anything else.

This time, when Edmond heard the excitement through his window, he thought how fun singing, dancing, and talking with friends must be. But shy Edmond had never been to a party, so he had no idea what one was really like.

Harry's next party was just a few days away.

Excited by the big news, Ant gave Harry a call.
"Is it true there's going to be a tart?" Ant asked.
"Absolutely," answered Harry, thinking to himself, *Mmm...a tart...*
"How wonderful," said Ant. "What kind will it be?"
"A nothing tart, I think. Those are by far the best," said Harry.

Ant's mouth began to water. *Yum, yum. A nothing tart…how mysterious!*

On his way home from collecting pinecones for a camel costume, George stopped by Harry's with a question of his own:
"Is it a costume party?" he asked hopefully.
"Could be," said Harry, still thinking about the tart. Then he told George that the evening would be absolutely unforgettable because of the wonderful nothing tart.

What costume will go best with a nothing tart? George wondered.

The night of the party arrived at last, and a crowd gathered at the foot of the old chestnut tree.

This time, Edmond really wanted to go. Just to see. *But I really shouldn't,* he thought. *That's a crazy idea. I'll just make a little jam instead.* He arranged his things at the stove and opened the window so he could hear the party.

The music wafting up from Harry's was cheerful, but Edmond didn't feel that way at all. He felt a bit lonely. Maybe even very lonely. So lonely, in fact, that his eyes began to fill with tears, which ran down into the pot. Not wanting his salty tears to ruin the jam, Edmond quickly closed the window and got into bed.

But the minute he turned off the light, there was a knock at the door.

It was Mr. George Owl, who had smelled the delicious aroma coming from Edmond's window.

Edmond told George it was from the pot of jam cooking on the stove. He didn't want to boast, but as he gave George some bread and jam, Edmond admitted that jam was something he knew how to make.

"Mmm," George said, licking his lips. "This jam is a true delicacy! Now I feel like dancing more than ever. Disguised, of course, as either a whale or a seagull. How about you?"

"Hmm… I'm okay," said Edmond.

"That's a shame!" George exclaimed. "Well, never mind. Stay as you are, and I'll just pretend you're disguised as a squirrel. But please, you must come and dance at the party, all right?"

It took no time at all for Edmond to pack up what was left of the nut jam and put on his pompom hat and for George to get into his seagull costume.

Then they were at Harry's!

Harry was delighted to meet Edmond.
"How splendid that you've come with a seagull!" he
exclaimed, completely unaware that it was George.

The party continued late into the night. Edmond danced with Ladybug and talked with Harry. Between bites of nothing tart, Ant asked the seagull what the vast emptiness of sea and sky was like. (Because it's so mysterious…this emptiness!)

And the seagull asked the other guests to tell him about Mr.
George Owl. (Because he's so mysterious...this George!) Then
everyone had a good laugh when Edmond told them that earlier
in the evening he had wept salty tears into his jam pot.
"But I don't think that will happen again," he smiled.

It was late when Edmond and George left the party.

George felt too awake to go right to sleep, so he decided to stay outside and enjoy his costume just a little longer. It looked so beautiful in the moonlight. As he gazed out at the night sky, George thought how pleasant the life of a seagull—a life of wind and waves—must be.

As for Edmond, for the first time in a long, long while, he went to bed without making any pompoms. Instead, he thought about George, Ant, and Harry, and how maybe the next party could be at his house for a change.

What if a zebra were to show up? That would be a real surprise! He would definitely have a word or two with George in the morning.

No matter what, he would make nut jam for everyone and pompoms, too.

Snug in his bed, Edmond smiled. Being surrounded by friends was surely what suited him best of all.

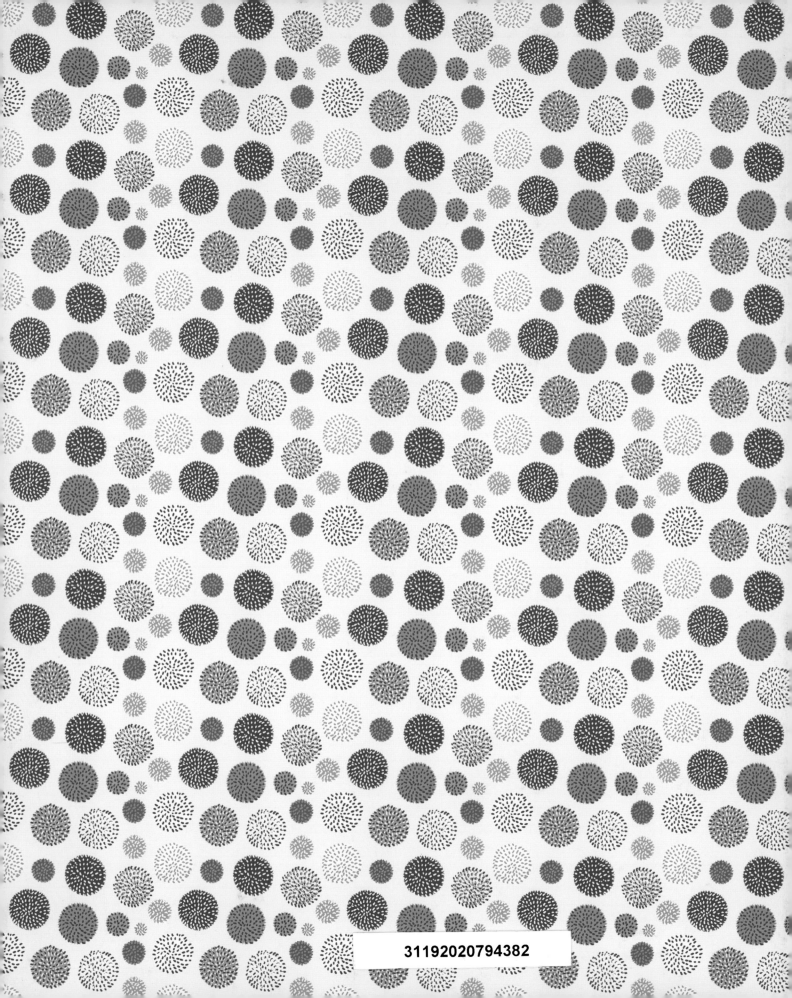

31192020794382